SESAME STREET

the MONSTER at the end of this book

written by *Jon Stone*
illustrated by *Mike Smollin*

Featuring Jim Henson's Sesame Street Muppets

A GOLDEN BOOK • NEW YORK
Golden Books Publishing Company, Inc., Racine, Wisconsin 53404

Published by Golden Books Publishing Company, Inc., in cooperation with Children's Television Workshop

A portion of the money you pay for this book goes to Children's Television Workshop. It is put right back into SESAME STREET and other CTW educational projects. Thanks for helping!

This is a very dull page. What is on the next page?

Maybe you do not understand.
You see, turning pages will
bring us to the end of
this book, and there is a
Monster at the end of
this book...

...but **this** will stop you from turning pages. See? I am tying the pages together so you cannot....

ALL RIGHT!! ALL RIGHT!! ALL RIGHT!!

Do you know that every time you turn another page . . . you not only get us closer to the MONSTER at the end of this book, but you make a Terrible mess!

The next page is the <u>end</u> of this book, and there is a **MONSTER** at the end of this book.

Oh, I am so **SCARED** !

Well, look at that! This is the end of the book, and the only one here is ...

ME

I, lovable, furry old **GROVER**, am the Monster at the end of this book.

And _you_ were so SCARED!

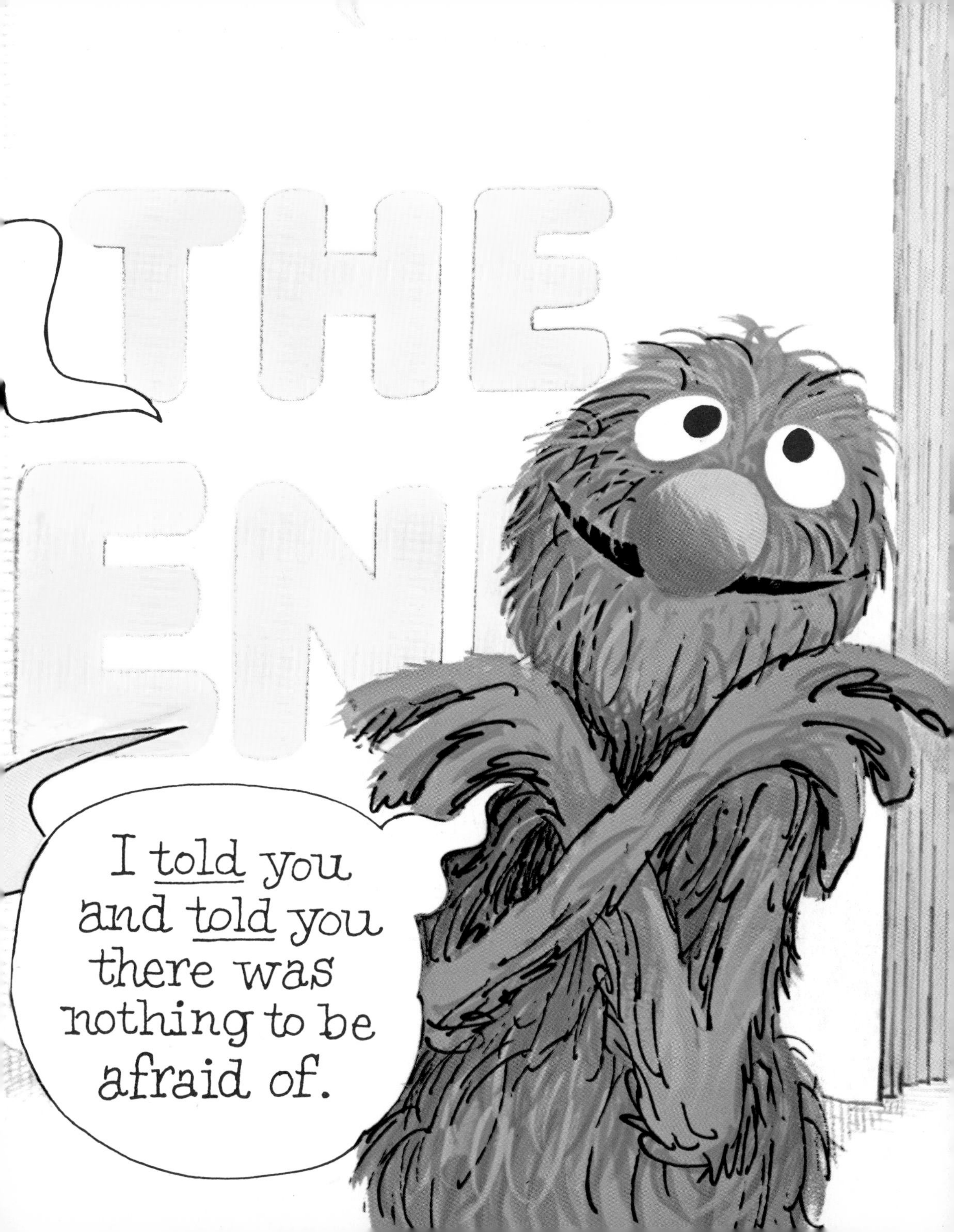
THE
I told you and told you there was nothing to be afraid of.